HEIDI

Four adventures based on Johanna Spyri's classic tale.

A Terrifying Grandfather

Grandmother's Old Chalet

Clara's Little Kittens

Heidi's Violin

TREASURE PRESS

First published in Great Britain in 1986 by
Treasure Press
59 Grosvenor Street
London W1

English Translation by Samuel Carr
Illustrations by Solvej Crevelier

Illustrations © Editions Lito, Paris
English translation © Octopus Books Ltd, 1986

ISBN 1 85051 060 1

Printed in Czechoslovakia
50585

A terrifying grandfather

The village of Maïenfeld nestles in the hollow of a pleasant valley. The village's only street turns into a road wide enough for the carts which make their way among the fields. Then this road narrows and becomes a steep path which climbs up towards the alpine pastures.

Along this path two people were briskly walking. One was a well-built young woman, the other a child scarcely five years old who found it difficult to trot along the stony surface. The hot June sun brought out the scent of the plants and the flowers; all the same, the little girl was wearing a woollen dress and over it a shawl, just as though it was winter.

'Are you tired, Heidi?' asked the woman.

'No, Aunt Dete, but I'm hot.'

'One more effort. If you stretch your little legs we shall be up there in less than an hour.'

Half-way up the slope they could see the little village of Dörfli. There Dete was born; she knew everyone there and several of her friends asked her to stop for a moment for a chat. But Dete said she was sorry; she had to hurry.

'It's such a nice day', said a plump and cheerful young woman who lived in the last house in the village. 'I'll come part of the way with you. I'd like to go up there too.'

'Come along then, Barbel, but don't delay us.'

The two friends set off at a good pace, with Heidi trailing along behind them. Their tongues wagged as fast as their legs were moving! They had such a lot of things to talk over: everything that had happened during the two months since they had last seen one another.

'But who is this pretty little creature, Dete? Isn't she the little orphan you look after?'

'That's right, Barbel. She is Heidi. My poor sister left her to us when she died. I have brought her up until now; but the time has come when I can do so no longer.'

'I see. But why not, Dete?'

'Let me explain. Last year, as you know, when Mother died, I went down to Ragaz to work as a chambermaid in a hotel. On my floor some very nice people from Frankfurt were staying. They have returned this year and they suggested to me that I should go back with them and work for them full time. Isn't it wonderful?'

'Yes, indeed. But what are you going to do with the little one?'

'Last year at Ragaz Heidi and I boarded with Ursula Pfäffer; but now that I'm leaving for Frankfurt this arrangement is no longer possible. So I'm taking her to my Uncle. She will stay with him.'

'Dete, you're crazy. One thing I'm sure of: the old man will send you packing, you and your schemes.'

'He really must look after her. I have done everything I could for the little girl because I promised Mother I would. But now it's up to the old man to take over. After all, he is the nearest thing to a parent Heidi has.'

'I see. I would rather not be in the little girl's shoes. The old man will treat her badly. Anyone would suppose you don't know him – this dreadful "Uncle of the Alps". But how was it that he came to get such a nickname?'

'Don't ask me everything at once; let me sort out my ideas. I know a good many things about the Uncle that I would not like everyone in the valley to know.'

'Don't you believe I can keep a secret?' Barbel asked, frowning.

The two young women drew closer together and Barbel linked her arm with her friend's. They wanted to be able to talk privately together. Heidi left them without a sound and allowed them to go on ahead.

'I say, look at your little girl. She has joined Peter, the little goatherd. That's best, after all; he will look after her better than we can. . . . Dete, dear, tell me about the Uncle. Has he always been such a beast?'

'To tell you the truth, I know nothing about it. I am only twenty-six, and he is at least seventy. But my Mother, who was born like him at Domleschg, has often spoken to me about him, and not too favourably either, believe you me.'

'Is he rich?'

'He inherited the big estate of Domleschg. But instead of working, he preferred to play at being a gentleman and to visit the gambling casinos. That killed his parents.'

'Is he an only son, then?'

'No, he did have a younger brother who was more serious and

sensible than he was. This brother disappeared after the bankruptcy and the Uncle too left the country. He was not seen again until, fifteen years later, he returned to Domleschg together with a young boy called Tobias. He wanted to present him to his family, but all doors were shut against him.'

'How was that?'

'People distrusted him. It was known that he had served as a soldier at Naples and that his wife, who was from the Grisons district of Switzerland, had died soon after Tobias was born. It was also said that he had killed a man in Naples, not in war but in a brawl, and that he had deserted from the army.'

'Do you know why he is called "Uncle"?'

'That's easily answered. Here in the valley we are all more or less related to one another. That's how he came to be called the Uncle of the Alp, because he lives up there.'

'But what happened to Tobias?'

'He apprenticed the boy to a carpenter. And, furious at the reception he had met with, he determined never to set foot in

the village of Dörfli again as long as he lived.'

'And Tobias?'

'Give me time to breathe, Barbel! Tobias was a fine boy, gentle and a good worker. My sister had loved him for a long time and he loved her. They were happy together, especially when their baby was born. But alas, hardly two months later Tobias was killed by the fall of a balk of timber in his carpenter's yard! Poor Adelaïde never recovered. She too was buried a few weeks after Tobias. It was a tragedy and the people of Dörfli said it came about as a punishment for the old man's godlessness. The village priest reproached him, but Uncle would not listen. He became still more unsociable. He settled down in the Alp and never wanted to leave it.'

'Dete, surely you aren't going to leave Heidi with the Uncle?'

'What else is there to do? I can't take a little girl of five with me to Frankfurt.'

The two friends were now half way up to the Alp.

'I stop here', Barbel said. 'I must talk to Peter's mother, who lives there, in that chalet. In the winter she does knitting for me. Good-bye, Dete, and good luck.'

The young woman sat down at the side of the path to wait until the two children caught up with her. After ten minutes she began to grow uneasy, when they were still not to be seen. At last she saw them pass the chalet on their way to rejoin her.

'But where have you been? And Heidi, whatever have you done with your Sunday dress? Where are your new shoes, and the stockings I knitted for you?'

'It was so hot, Aunt Dete; I took them off.'

And the little girl pointed her finger at a coloured heap of clothes, clearly visible in contrast to the deep green of the meadow.

'Now will you tell me why you took your things off?'

'I didn't need them any more. Oh, Aunt Dete, we had such a good time together, Peter and I. Every day he looks after the goats and his mother calls him the goatherd. He has a grand-mother too, and he knows all the mountain paths.'

'You had better be quiet, you little chatterbox. And you, you rascal, don't stand there like an idiot, but run as fast as you can to look for the clothes.'

'I'm late already', the little goatherd replied, his two fists stuck into the pockets of his trousers.

'Don't go on staring at me with those round eyes. If you run fast I'll give you this lovely new halfpenny.'

The young scamp had never possessed such a treasure. He dashed off down the hill and was soon back with the bundle under his arm. Dete congratulated him.

'And now you might as well come up with us to Uncle. Carry this parcel; that will help us.'

And the little party set off for Uncle's chalet. Peter cracked his whip while the goats and Heidi danced happily round him. The chalet stood high up on a spur of the hills, exposed to the sun and to every wind that blows. From there the whole valley could be seen. At its back, a small plantation of firs gave a little shade, then the meadow sloped up again until it reached a wall of bare rock. On a bench sat the old man, smoking his pipe and watching the arrival of his visitors.

A few yards from the chalet Heidi began to run so as to be the first to reach him.

'Good evening, Grandfather.'

The old man stared at her from under his thick, grey eyebrows. He muttered to himself as he turned to watch her cheeky approach.

'Hey, what's that you're saying?'

The little girl wasn't to be put off by the old man's unkempt beard, his surly air and his mistrustful look. Meanwhile Dete had arrived. Peter stood apart, watching to see what was going to happen.

'Good-day, Uncle', said Dete. 'I've brought you Heidi. She is Tobias and Adelaïde's daughter. I'm sure that you won't recognise her after all this time...'

'Oh, and why do you bring her to me?'

('What are you doing there', he said to the boy. 'You're late already with the goats. Take mine too whilst you are about it.')

The little goatherd made off at once without even asking for a rest. He could tell from his look that the old man wasn't in a joking mood.

'I have had her for four years', continued Dete. 'It's your turn now.'

'I see. And what if the little girl doesn't like me and starts to cry. ...'

'That's your business, not mine. Did anyone help me when she was a babe in arms, hardly a year old, and when I had my mother to look after too? Now I can't do any more. You are the nearest there is to a parent for her. If she is badly cared for it will

be your fault – and that won't be the only thing you will have to reproach yourself with!'

After saying these terrible words, Dete felt rather uneasy. She had said more than she meant to. But she could not unsay the words as the old man looked at her steadily. Startled, she retreated a pace or two.

The Grandfather rose to his feet.

'Off you go! Go back to where you came from, but don't ever come back here again!'

Dete did not give him time to repeat what he had said. She turned on her heels and fled.

'Good-bye, Uncle, Good-bye, Heidi', she cried.

She ran right through the village of Dörfli without replying to the questions people were asking her.

'What have you done with the little girl?'

'Have you left her with the Uncle, up there?'

Dete continued on her way, worried by the thoughts that kept repeating themselves in her head. 'Poor little thing, with no one to help her at the Uncle's. It's a bad business.'

Dete ran faster to stifle the voice of conscience. After all, she had promised her mother that she would never abandon Heidi.

'I'll look after her later when I've earned some money', she said to herself.

But in reality Dete's only thought was to escape as fast as she could from the valley where everyone knew about everything she did, and to get to the big city. There she would at least be left in peace.

After Dete had gone, the Grandfather returned to his seat on the bench and, silently, puffed big clouds of white smoke from his pipe. Heidi walked right round the chalet and up to the old fir trees. But as the wind blew so strongly and made such a noise in the branches, she returned to the old man.

'I'd like to see your house, Grandfather.'

'Off you go then. But take your bundle of clothes with you.'

'I don't need them now.'

'How is that?'

'I'd rather walk bare-legged like the goats.'

'You're quite right. But take your clothes just the same. We must put them away.'

The chalet was poorly furnished. In one corner was Grandfather's bed and opposite it was the fire-place with its big cooking-pot. There were also a table, a chair and a cupboard. Grandfather opened the door of the cupboard. His socks and shirts didn't take up much space; there was still plenty of room on the shelves for Heidi's clothes.

'Where do you sleep, Grandfather?'

'There, in that bed.'

'And me?'

'Where you like.'

This answer suited the little girl very well.
She had noticed a ladder leading to the hay-
loft and, laughing, she climbed up to the
very top.

'I'm going to sleep here, Grandfather.
And when I wake up I shall see the sun in
the valley.'

'Fine, that's agreed then. But I'm going
to lay this sack on the hay to keep the straw
from tickling your nose.'

Suddenly Heidi remembered that she had
had nothing to eat since morning: only a
little coffee and a slice of bread and butter.

'I'm hungry, Grandfather.'

The old man lit a fire of sticks under the pot. Heidi watched him for a moment or two, then she decided to help. She laid the table with two plates and forks; but as there was only one glass, she took a cup for herself from the hanging shelves.

The old man watched her at work out of the corner of his eye. He was pleased to see that his little girl was so wide-awake. Then Heidi said,

'I've no chair to sit on, Grandfather.'

'To-day you must eat standing up, but after we have eaten I shall make you a stool.'

The old man found a little plank of wood of about the right thickness in his wood-shed. In it he bored three holes into which he inserted the stool's legs. The little girl was amazed at how skilful the old man was.

Already evening was coming on ... When it was dusk, Peter the goatherd appeared with his flock. Heidi was happy to see him and ran to meet him. A beautiful white goat, and another one that was black and smaller, separated themselves from the flock. They trotted off in the direction of Uncle, who waited for them, a fistful of salt in the palm of his rough hand.

The two goats greedily licked up the salt.

'Aren't they pretty? The dark one there is called Blackie, and the name of the other one is Snowflake.'

In another moment or two, Grandfather had milked the two goats and Heidi was drinking from a big bowl of fresh milk which gave her a white moustache. Never had she tasted anything so good.

The little girl said to herself that her terrifying Grandfather was really very nice and that she would be happy with him and the goats up there on the Alp.

Uncle got supper ready and Heidi laid the table again as she had done at mid-day. But now she did not have to eat standing up. Perched on her new stool, she sat opposite her Grandfather and smiled at him.

'That's delicious. I was really hungry.'

'It's the effect of good mountain air. But tell me: are you afraid to sleep all alone in the hay-loft, with the noisy wind we have this evening?'

'Not me. Quick, let's finish the meal and I'll go upstairs to bed.'

In the middle of the night Uncle woke up.

'This storm will stop her from sleeping', he said to himself.

Silently, he climbed the rungs of the ladder and slipped his head through the trap-door. It was a clear night and he could see Heidi, who was sleeping like an angel. A moonbeam shone down on her and she was smiling, as if she was having beautiful dreams.

The old man lay down on his bed once more and fell asleep again, moved by what he had seen. The coming of this sweet little girl had completely changed his life. In future the chalet was to resound with laughter and song.

Grandmother's old chalet

Heidi woke up early and dressed herself at once. She was in a hurry to see her Grandfather again; he was busy with Snowflake and Blackie. Peter, the goatherd, was already there with the goats of his own flock.

'Good morning, Grandfather. I've had a good sleep.'

'Then you will certainly want to go to the pasture with the General of the Goats.'

'General? What General?'

'Peter. He commands the creatures like a true leader. But if you want to go with him you will first have to wash your face.'

Without further ado Heidi splashed fresh water over her face and arms; then she rubbed herself hard with a towel to get warm.

When the two children left the chalet, the sun was shining in a wonderful blue sky. The weather was marvellous. The butterflies fluttered from flower to flower and the little girl followed them, running first to one side, then to the other. But Peter was worried.

'Watch out, Heidi; don't run just anywhere. You would hurt yourself badly if you fell on a rock.'

By knotting together the four corners of her apron, Heidi made a carrier into which she put all the flowers she picked. Never had she enjoyed herself so much. Peter, like someone who knows how to save his energy, hung his haversack on the low branch of a dead tree. Then he lay full length on the grass, in the shade, to have a sleep.

When he woke up it was already time to eat. Peter didn't have a watch, but by simply seeing where the sun was in the sky, he could tell what time it was.

'Hey there, Heidi. Stop for a moment or you'll tire yourself

out running about. We're going to have our lunch.'

'Oh, what a good idea, Peter. I'm dying of hunger.'

The boy lifted down his haversack and took from it the big slices of bread and the cheese which Grandfather put in it every day. But to-day the slices were thicker and the children took big bites out of them.

'Are you thirsty, Heidi?'

'Yes, but Grandfather has forgotten to give us anything to drink. There *is* an empty bowl in the haversack. What shall we do?'

'We've everything we need to fill that bowl. Blackie, Blackie, come here.'

The goat softly approached. *She* knew why he was called the General. Peter milked the goat and offered Heidi a big bowl of warm, creamy milk. She drank it up with keen pleasure.

'Here, Peter,' she said, holding out what remained of her bread and butter. 'Do take it. I'm not hungry any more.'

'Oh no, Heidi. I ought not. Uncle made it for you. He would not be pleased.'

'Please, please, have it. I'd like you to.'

The General of the Goats did not need to be asked twice. He was always as hungry as a hunter and it was a long time since he had had such a feast. It was a meal fit for a king!

All this time Heidi was examining the goats and was trying to memorise their names. Now she was able to recognise all of them.

There was Turk, the strongest of them. He had formidable horns and a wicked nature. He stayed a little apart from the rest of the flock. The others dared not go near him. Only Greenfinch, a pretty female goat with delicate long legs, did not seem to be afraid of him and dared to oppose him. And there was Matilda, who never stopped butting, and Daisy, who ran so gracefully. She was Peter's favourite. For Heidi the two queens of the flock were Snowflake and Blackie, Grandfather's two goats.

The afternoon passed quickly and Heidi did not notice the hours fly by. However, it grew cooler and the sun sank behind the high rocks. Soon the sky was lit up by the splendid red rays of the sun.

'Peter, there must be a fire!'

'No, Heidi. It's only the sun hiding behind the clouds.'

'Why?'

'Well, I'm not sure. It's like that every evening. Come on. It's time to go home now.'

And, led by its General, the little party cheerfully made for the chalet. Seated on his bench, Grandfather watched the children return.

'Hullo there, Heidi. Have you been enjoying yourself?'

'Oh yes. It's wonderful up there. I ran after the butterflies. There was a fire on the rocks. Peter told me it was the sun. I've picked lots of flowers. Hundreds of them. Just look!'

Heidi undid the corners of her apron. But what a disappointment! Only sad, withered stalks fell to the ground. The little girl felt like crying; whatever had happened to her pretty bouquet?

'Don't worry, dear. It was very kind of you to want to bring me back some flowers; but up there, you see, they're just like us. In taking them away from the sun and the pure air you have deprived them of life. They are dead.'

'I see, Grandfather. I won't pick them any more. I would

rather see them alive in all their lovely colours.'

'You are quite right. And now, run and have a wash. You have got yourself into a fine state, dashing about all day behind the goats. I'll see to Snowflake and Blackie while I'm waiting for you.'

Heidi did as she was told. She rubbed on the soap and splashed herself with the refreshing water. When she returned to her Grandfather she was shining like a new pin.

Next day, when Peter turned up at the usual time, Heidi was ready to set off with him. The little goatherd asked for nothing better than to lead the party. Heidi entertained him with her laughter and her odd questions; and, who knows, perhaps Uncle might put some bigger slices of bread and butter in the haversack because of Heidi . . .

In this way, day followed day in that lovely time of year. Heidi flourished in the pure mountain air. Her cheeks filled out and became rounded and the calves of her legs were firm and round too. But now autumn was drawing near. Each day the sun set a little earlier behind the black wall of the rocks, and at night the wind started up its fiendish dance once again.

The time had come to take the wool dress from the cupboard and to put on her thick, warm socks.

'You won't be able to go up into the mountain with Peter any longer, Heidi. It's far too cold now.'

The one who felt the most sad about this was the little goatherd. Without Heidi his meals became smaller, the bread and butter not so generous and the cheese less. As for the little girl, she wasn't too disappointed: her Grandfather wasn't idle for a moment and she followed him all round the house. She helped him to make the little goat's-milk cheeses, so round and

white. She watched him handling his saw, his file and his hammer; and when it began to grow dark in the room he used for his workshop, it was she who brushed up the sawdust and shavings.

One morning when she looked out of her window, Heidi's gaze was met by a shimmering white landscape. The first of the snow had fallen. It would soon be winter.

'Our General will be miserable. He will have to hang up his whip and exchange it for a pen.'

'Why a pen? He won't need one so long as he is a goatherd.'

'During the winter he must go to school to learn reading, writing and arithmetic. He doesn't like school: but he must go there just the same, Heidi.'

'So I won't be seeing Peter any more, Grandfather?' Heidi sounded disappointed.

'Oh, the snow won't stop him climbing up here if he is keen to see you.'

'I hope he will come!'

One afternoon, when Heidi and her Uncle were warming their hands in front of a big fire of fir-logs, there was a knock at the door.

'Open the door, my dear.'

'It's Peter! Good-morning, Peter!'

'You must be cold, my boy. Come nearer the fireplace. And perhaps you're hungry too; why don't Heidi and you have something to eat?'

The two friends sat down at the table in front of a big bowl of milk, some wholemeal bread and a piece of smoked meat. Between mouthfuls, the boy told Heidi what had been happening at school. She wanted to know everything, down to the last detail, including what class he was in and what games they played. Without seeming to listen, Grandfather followed their talk and was entertained by the children's chatter. When they were there his house was a cheerful place.

'Now, Peter, you must go back home again. Your Grandmother will be worried about you.'

'I'll come back again next week. But Grandmother would like to get to know you, Heidi. You must visit us.'

'Oh yes, Peter! I'd love to come.'

'Out of the question!' Grandfather interrupted. 'Out of the question. The weather is too bad and the snow is too thick. You would get lost.'

'But I should be very careful, Grandfather. Peter doesn't get lost. I'm big too.'

The snowstorm lasted for days and days. The big snowflakes whirled down during the night and every morning Uncle had to clear a path in front of the chalet door with his big, wide shovel.

Then, on the morning of the fifth day, Heidi clapped her hands with joy. The landscape was frozen, sparkling like a dress

covered in beautiful pearls and the sun was shining from a brilliant blue sky. The little girl jumped up and down with happiness.

'The fine weather has come, Grandfather. The fine weather has come. I'll visit Peter. You promised me I could.'

'All right, all right! Go, then, since you want to so much', grumbled the old man in a grudging voice.

He went out to the shed which served as the goats' stable and fetched an old sledge for two people. He sat down on it and, wrapping Heidi up in a warm blanket, set her down in front of him. With a good push from both his heels at once, he let off the brake and the runners began to cut through the snow with a cheerful squeal. The sledge slid along like the wind. The cold made Heidi's nose red, but she was in heaven. On each side of the track the frost-covered firs made a guard of honour for her. In a short while the sledge, expertly directed by the old man, had reached the chalet of the General of the Goats and softly came to rest on a flat piece of ground in front of the door.

'You've arrived, Heidi. You can stay with Peter all afternoon.

But promise me to start back before the sun begins to set.'

Heidi promised, and the old man gave her a hug: he was moved, but he did not want anyone to see. He quickly returned the way they had come, dragging the sledge behind him by a rope passed over his shoulder. Without waiting any longer, Heidi turned towards the house. She was in a hurry to get to know Peter's home and to meet his Mother and his Grand-mother.

She pushed open a door which creaked on its rusty hinges and found herself in a dark room. Her eyes grew used to the darkness and she could make out, in the corner, an earthenware stove on which there was a basin made of leather. Heidi walked across the room without pausing and opened a second door

41

which led to the main room of the house.

What a poverty-stricken place! Brigitte, Peter's mother, sat at a roughly-made wooden table mending her son's clothes. She had to bend low over the work as the daylight, shining through the dirty windows, was dim. Beside the fireplace an old woman was seated, working at a creaking spinning-wheel. Her face was as lined as an old apple and her hair was gathered under a linen cap.

Heidi knew at once that this was Peter's Grandmother and she went up close to her chair. The Grandmother, hearing the little girl's steps, stopped her work and held out her arms in welcome.

'Good-morning, Grandmother. I am Heidi, the General's friend. I hope you haven't been waiting for me too long?'

The old woman looked surprised.

'General? What general?'

'My Grandfather calls Peter that – it shows how good he is at leading his flock.'

'Are you the one who lives up in the Alp, then? The little girl Dete brought back to live with Uncle?'

'Yes. He brought me down on a big sledge.'

The Grandmother shook her head incredulously.

'Goodness me! I can't believe it! It's true, then, Brigitte, what Peter has been telling us. The whole village agreed that he would only keep the little girl for a fortnight; but she stayed on. It's a divine miracle, that it is. How does she look? Has she been well fed?'

Brigitte smiled.

'She has curly hair just like Adelaïde had, and her black eyes shine just as Tobias's used to. She seems to be in excellent health', she replied.

The little girl sat down near Grandmother's chair. She took the old woman's dry old hands in her own little ones.

'You can't see anything, then, Grandmother?'

'No, my dear. My poor eyes are so worn out, so sick, that everything round me is black.'

'No one can cure them?'

'No, my dear. I am blind.'

Heidi did not understand what this word meant, but she knew it stood for a grave illness and, as she was already fond of the Grandmother, she began to shed tears. Brigitte and Grandmother were much moved and they did what they could to console her.

'Isn't she sweet, the little one! And what a good heart she has!'

To bring back a smile to Heidi's lips, Grandmother told her some of the many stories she knew: about the fox, who crept one night into the hen-house at Dörfli; about the blue tit-mouse, who made her nest in a rowan-tree; and about Flicka, Hans's dog, whom his master had trained to carry a basket in his teeth with the mid-day meal in it. Heidi listened avidly. Through these tales that Grandmother told she learned to understand the life of the valley. Then the old woman talked about her old chalet, so old that one day it might collapse in a squall of wind. At night Peter slept soundly, but Grandmother found it hard to sleep, especially when the wind whistled through the cracks in the roof and made the rafters shake so much that she was afraid they might fall down.

'I shall ask my Grandfather if he will mend the house, Grandmother. He will come with his hammer and nails and he will stop up the holes. The wind won't be able to get in and you will be able to sleep in peace.'

Brigitte looked at the little girl with wondering eyes. What

she said suggested common sense beyond her years. She was as intelligent as a girl of twelve years old, and when she spoke of the days spent with the old man in the Alp, it was clear that she was happy. Her work with the goats and with cheese-making, and the long evenings passed in the chimney-corner while her Grandfather carved fine things from wood with his knife – you could see that all this gave her everything she wanted. Heidi talked on and on and was proud to find that she was listened to as though she was a grown-up.

'Who would have thought that of the Uncle?' the Grandmother exclaimed. 'How he has changed in only a few months!'

At this moment the door was opened with a bang. It was Peter, back from school and making the floor resound with his wooden clogs.

'You're back already', said Grandmother. 'You have got on well with your lessons, I hope.'

'Well . . .'

'Oh, Peter', said Brigitte, 'you are nearly thirteen and you are no further on than a boy of eight at the most.'

'You can't read my Bible or my prayer-book to me yet', sighed Grandmother.

'What's a Bible?' Heidi asked.

'A big book. I was given one the day I was married. In it are fine things to read, prayers and psalms. But now that my eyes are worn out it is no more use to me.'

It grew darker and darker in the room. Brigitte lit the oil lamp which stood on the chimney-piece and put it in the centre of the table.

'Oh, I must leave you. I promised my Grandfather.'

'Off you go at once, then, Heidi. You mustn't worry him. Peter will go with you to see you don't get lost in the snow. Now, wrap up warmly!'

Half an hour later the little goatherd was back and told them that Grandfather had come down the mountain to meet them. He had given Heidi a kiss and had asked her if she hadn't been too bored.

'It's a blessing', exclaimed Grandmother. 'I shall pray to God that the little girl will visit us again many times.'

Meanwhile the old man climbed up to his chalet again, carrying the sleeping girl in his strong arms. She was cosy like that, her nose hidden in the warm wool of her Grandfather's jersey. When they got to the chalet he set her down in front of the fire-place, blowing up the rosy embers.

'So you enjoyed yourself?'

'Yes, indeed, Grandfather. But I'd like to ask you something.'

'What is it now?'

'I want you to come down there with me and mend Grandmother's house.'

'What an idea!'

'Oh, Grandfather, their chalet is so old. One day it will tumble down on top of them.'

The good old man looked at his little girl. He was deeply moved and he kissed her on both cheeks.

'You are a good child. It's agreed, Heidi, we will go and do the job tomorrow.'

Heidi was so happy that she danced right round the room on one leg.

'Hey there, you'll burst my eardrums. Quick, drink up your soup and get to bed. You must be really tired.'

Next day the old man again placed the little girl in front of him on the sledge and away they went to Peter's chalet. Heidi ran into the room.

'Hullo there, Grandmother. I'm back. And I've got a big surprise for you. Listen. ...'

Dull blows echoed through the whole house.

'My goodness, whatever is happening? What's the meaning of that noise?'

'Don't worry, Grandmother. It's my Grandfather, who is mending the house.'

Brigitte was quite confused and left the room to thank the carpenter. She hardly knew what to say to him.

'Spare me your chatter, Brigitte, or I won't be finished before dark.'

And Brigitte left him. She well knew that he wasn't as bad as he liked to appear.

By the evening all the faulty boards in the roof had been mended.

'Heidi', the old man called out in a loud voice. 'Heidi, it's time we went back home.'

'You must go, my dear', said Grandmother. It wouldn't do to make him wait. *You* will thank Uncle for us.'

And just as she had done the day before, Heidi returned in the arms of her Grandfather as he dragged behind him the sledge, sliding along on its steel runners.

In the chalet, into which the wind could no longer enter, the Grandmother never tired of saying:

'It is a miracle. It is the blessing of God.'

Clara's little kittens

In only a few months Heidi had become a real little girl of the Alp. She understood how to give orders to Blackie and Snowflake as well as did Peter, the General of the Goats. Grandfather was proud to discover that little Heidi could help him in all sorts of ways. The chalet was looked after like a real home. Everything was clean and in its proper place. Heidi was a true housewife. How happy she was, up there in the mountains!

She often went down to Grandmother's chalet, listening all afternoon to her wonderful stories and never failing to return to Uncle's chalet before it grew dark.

But Heidi didn't go to school. All she knew was what the Grandfather taught her: the names of the trees, the flowers and the birds. She became really learned when it came to things of the mountain. But she could not read a book! One day Aunt Dete paid a visit to the chalet.

'How beautiful she is and how smartly dressed', thought Heidi, watching her as she arrived.

She was wearing a hat like those of town ladies. The old man looked at her in a very unfriendly way. He had not forgotten how she had abandoned Heidi, leaving her on his hands when she had decided to go to Frankfurt. Why had she come back, and what did she want now?

Dete realized that the old man awaited her with mistrust. She tried to get round him with flattery.

'Good-day, Uncle. I'm told that Heidi is being looked after

like a princess. It's certainly true that she looks well and that she seems to be happy with you. I'm very grateful to you, Uncle, for everything you have done for the child.'

And Dete reminded them that she had had to leave Heidi because of the job she had been offered at Frankfurt. She could not take Heidi with her, otherwise she would have done so. But now things were different.

'Where do you want to take her', asked the old man crossly. 'Tell me quickly what you have to say and let's have done with it.'

Dete was taken aback by Grandfather's fierce tone.

Taking her courage in both hands, she quickly explained that in Frankfurt she had got to know some very nice people, cousins of those she worked for. Herr Sesemann, the cousin in question, was a rich, kind man. He was a widower with one not very strong little girl, and he hoped to find a companion with whom his child could share her work and play.

'So I mentioned Heidi', went on Dete. 'The Sesemanns accepted my offer immediately. They would like to welcome Heidi as soon as possible. It's a marvellous opportunity, Uncle.'

'I've nothing to say to that', the old man replied.

'You'd rather Heidi grew up like a little savage, then? I know you won't take her to church or allow her to go to school. By what right do you prevent her from mixing with children of her own age?'

'You annoy me, Dete, with your airs and graces.'

'Well, all I can say is that Heidi is my poor sister's daughter. I am responsible for her and I won't leave without her.'

Heidi listened anxiously to the quarrel. She was not used to people raising their voices. Aunt Dete seemed like a stranger to her in her town clothes. She no longer belonged to the mountains.

Heidi had never seen her Grandfather so angry before. The old man marched about the room with a flushed face and upraised arms.

'All right, then. If that's how you feel off you go with the child. But don't come back here in a hurry.' And he stamped out of the chalet, leaving the little girl and her Aunt Dete alone.

Dete made up a parcel of all Heidi's things – not a very big one, it's true.

'Let's go now,' she said. 'At once.'

'I don't want to go with you, Aunt Dete. I don't love you, and

Grandfather is so angry!' Heidi said unhappily.

'Don't worry. He will calm down when he is by himself. You really don't want to come with me, Heidi? Just think: we shall take the train and have a lovely trip. At Frankfurt you will see all the fine houses and the splendid shops. Come along, now. I've no time to lose.'

'Yes, but I'd like to go back to the chalet and see Grandfather again.'

'You'll soon come back. It's easy by train.'

Reassured by this false promise, the little girl allowed herself to be led away by Dete and off they hurried down the slope as fast as they could go.

When they grew level with Grandmother's chalet Heidi hung back a little.

'Let's stop, Aunt Dete. I would like to say hullo to Grandmother.'

'We haven't got the time. Quick; don't hold me up like this. We shall buy some soft, white rolls at Frankfurt. They are delicious. You can bring them back to Grandmother. They are just the thing for her old teeth.'

'Oh yes, Aunt Dete' the little girl said, excited at the idea. 'Let's run so that we won't miss the train.'

Innocent little Heidi believed everything her Aunt told her and would have followed her to the end of the earth.

Seeing the young woman leading the child breathlessly along, the people of Dörfli asked themselves what the reason for this hurry could be.

'Has the old man been treating the child badly', they wondered, 'since her Aunt has had to come back for her?' 'Oh Dete, where are you off to so fast? Is the old man after you?'

Dete didn't answer them but hurried on down the valley.

As for Grandfather, he sat sorrowfully and angrily on the bench in front of his chalet. Without Heidi he had lost all interest in living, and he hated the whole world!

Clara Sesemann lived in a big, beautiful stone house in Frankfurt – such a house as Heidi had never seen before. Clara was not well and her legs were not strong enough to support her. She went from room to room in a wheelchair. This was the way in which she moved along the waxed wooden floor from the dining room to the library where the books, bound in leather and lettered in gold, were lined up on polished oak shelves. In the drawing room her favourite toys were spread about over the costly rugs.

It was in the library that a tutor gave Clara her lessons. Clara was as blonde as Heidi was dark-haired and as pale as the little

mountain girl was hale and hearty. Her delicate face was framed by long ringlets tied up in red ribbons.

Her father, rich Herr Sesemann, often had to be away on business. So it came about that the housekeeping and his daughter's education had been placed in the hands of Fräulein Emma Rottenmeier, a tall, dry, stern woman who was always encased in a tight black dress and whose hair was pulled severely back. Emma Rottenmeier was severe and strict. However, she was very fond of Clara and did everything she could to see that she was properly educated. Herr Sesemann had every reason to rely on her. Nothing escaped her notice and everyone obeyed her slightest word.

Therefore, Emma Rottenmeier had complete freedom to choose a little friend for Clara. Dete had given her so favourable an account of Heidi that she was sure she had made a good choice, and she was looking forward eagerly to meeting Clara's new companion.

After a pleasant train journey, Dete and Heidi arrived at Frankfurt when night had already fallen. They hurried to find the house of Herr Sesemann.

Soon the two of them were at the front door and Dete was firmly pressing the bell. There was some delay in answering it. At last a servant half-opened the door.

'What is going on here? This is no time to disturb decent people.'

'Fräulein Rottenmeier is expecting us', said Dete.

'Well, that's not my affair. It's Elizabeth's business. I'll go and find her.'

Pressing herself fearfully against her Aunt's skirt, Heidi wondered what this reception could mean and why the large gentleman had had to ask Elizabeth for permission to allow them to come in.

At last a young woman appeared and asked in a rather more friendly tone:

'What do you want?'

'I know it's late', Dete replied, 'but I think that we must trouble Fräulein Rottenmeier.'

'Please follow me.'

Holding Heidi by the hand, the maid Elizabeth – for it was she – then led Dete up a big flight of steps. She opened the library door and stood back so as to let her visitors pass through it. Once inside, Heidi opened her eyes wide at the decoration on the panelling and at the unfamiliar books. Clara was sitting in her wheelchair at the further end of the room and was looking with the greatest curiosity at the little friend whom she had been promised and who had at last arrived.

With a stiff and majestic step, Emma Rottenmeier approached her visitors.

'What is your name, my dear?'

'Heidi.'

The governess raised her eyebrows.

'Heidi! That is no name for a Christian. By what name were you baptised?'

'I don't know,' replied the little girl, jumping from one foot to the other and looking as if she didn't understand the question.

Seeing that there was the risk of a misunderstanding, Dete broke in.

'Please forgive her, Fräulein. She is a little confused after the long journey and she doesn't understand town manners. Her real name is Adelaïde, but we call her Heidi. It is a pet name which is common where we come from.'

'I prefer Adelaïde. And how old is she? She seems to me younger than Clara. I made it clear that I was hoping to find a companion of her own age for her.'

'She *is* a little young, Fräulein. She is getting on for ten.'

'Oh no, Aunt Dete. I'm eight. Grandfather told me so and he never makes a mistake.'

'Eight! It's a disaster, Dete. And what does she know? What have you learned at school?'

'Nothing, Madam. Grandfather wouldn't allow me to go to school.'

'You have deceived me. This is not at all what we had agreed. What kind of friend will an ignorant little girl like that make for Clara?'

Dete could see that things were taking a dangerous turn and, if she was not to have to take her niece back to Grandfather, it was time to beat a retreat.

Making a deep curtsey, she hurriedly took her leave, saying she was sure that the two little girls would get on splendidly together, and that she really had to go. She had hardly finished speaking when Fräulein Rottenmeier realized that she had left the little girl behind and ran off after her, but too late. Dete was gone.

Left alone in the library, the two children looked at one another smilingly – the invalid with long, blonde curls, the little savage brown and sunburned.

'What name would you like me to call you by, Adelaïde or Heidi?' Clara asked.

'Heidi.'

'I'm very pleased you have come, Heidi. I'm sure we shall get on well together.'

For Heidi, however, the first days at Frankfurt produced a series of disasters.

The first of Heidi's blunders happened at supper the very first day she arrived. Seeing fat Gaspard the butler, arrayed in his fancy waistcoat and shirt-front, Heidi couldn't stop herself saying:

'You're just like the Goats' General when he is wearing his Sunday clothes.'

On hearing this outrageous remark, Fräulein Rottenmeier drew herself up and exclaimed:

'Goodness gracious! This naughty child is talking to the servants!'

A little later Heidi, realising that the small piece of bread on her plate was really hers, hastened to hide it in the pocket of her apron.

'That's for Grandmother', she said.

Clara had seen what had happened and exploded with laughter; but it wasn't cruel laughter. She just thought that Heidi was fun and that now meal-times would no longer be such gloomy, boring occasions as they had been in the past.

Next morning Heidi woke up in a pretty bedroom whose walls were covered in flowered paper. She dashed to the window and pressed her nose against the panes. But there she had a sad disappointment: instead of the laughing valley of Dörfli there were only cold, grey walls. It was with a heavy heart that she was

shown to the dining room for breakfast. Luckily, Clara welcomed her there with a sweet smile.

At a quarter to ten the tutor arrived, as he did every day at exactly the same time. Heidi opened her eyes wide at the sight of this curious being, small and thin and wearing a black frock coat and a grey hat. He had come to give Clara her lessons, those famous lessons in which Heidi was now to take part. Less than a quarter of an hour later a tremendous din shook the library. It was Heidi, who had been up to her tricks again. Hearing an unfamiliar noise in the street, she had run to the window, getting caught up in the tablecloth on the way and upsetting onto the floor the notebooks, the pens . . . and the ink-pot.

But compared to what was to happen with the cats, that was nothing.

Heidi hadn't forgotten the mountains, the Grandmother to whom she must bring the white rolls, and the chalet where her Grandfather was waiting for her. But where were these mountains? She would have to climb up, up, to the top of a big tower, so that she could see them over the roofs of the houses.

Taking advantage of the deep silence which reigned in the house after the mid-day meal, the little girl opened the front door and slipped out into the street. What an extraordinary sight met her eyes! Ladies, wearing hats even stranger than her Aunt Dete's, were walking along with little dogs on leads. Smartly dressed gentlemen hurried about with a dissatisfied

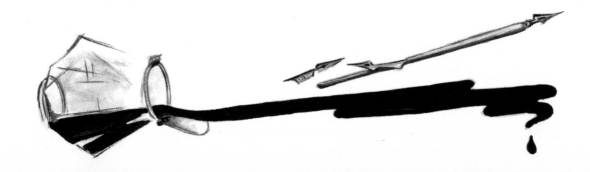

look on their faces. In the middle of the street the carriages rolled along with a noise like thunder.

Heidi hesitated for a long time before trusting herself to join such a throng. Then she made up her mind and crossed to the other side of the street, turned right at random, and crossed a big square where she was surprised to see a cloud of grey pigeons rise up at her approach.

Beside a pillar, a boy, who was scarcely bigger than she was herself, watched her draw near. Next to him stood a beautiful carved and gilded box and on it was a strange, smooth animal with a sharp-pointed head.

'Good-day', said Heidi. 'What kind of animal is that you have?'

The boy burst out laughing.

'It's a tortoise of course.'

'And the box?'

'You really don't know? It's a hurdy-gurdy. I can make music by turning its handle. Would you like me to? Then you must give me some pennies.'

'I don't have any pennies. But Clara will give you some money if you bring me to a big, high tower.'

'A big, high tower? I don't know it. But near here there's a church with a tall belfry.'

'Take me to it and you will get another two pennies.'

The organ-grinder thought the little girl odd but sweet, and he led her to the entrance to the belfry. As it was closed, he had to pull several times on the bell-rope before the caretaker would come.

'What do you want, you scamps?' he grumbled.

'I'd like to climb up the tower, Sir' said Heidi.

'It's out of the question now. Where are your mother and father, my dear?'

Touched by the tone of the old man's voice, Heidi felt a big sob rise in her throat. In spite of her tears, however, she went on looking at the caretaker.

The old man was not unkind. He pitied her because she seemed so sad.

'All right, come along then.'

And he led them up a long, long flight of steps to the very top. There he took her up in his arms so that she could see the view at her ease. But Heidi was disappointed. She thought she would be able to see the chalet in the Alp, but all she could make out was a sea of blue roofs ending in a forest.

On the way down she heard the sound of mewing coming from a garret situated in the tower.

'It sounds like cats, Sir.'

'Yes, my dear. My grey cat has just had kittens. Would you like to see them?'

Heidi was delighted at the sight of the little grey balls of fur moving around at the bottom of a wicker basket. She wanted to touch them, but their mother rose up and showed her claws.

'Leave her to me,' said the caretaker. 'I'll calm her. She knows me. If you like, I'll give you two of the kittens. You need only pop them in your apron pocket.'

The kind man had a further idea!

'Why don't I give them *all* to you?' (Like that, he thought to himself, I won't have to drown them).

The little girl clapped her hands. The kittens were so sweet. And Clara, who often found time lie heavy on her hands, would be so pleased at having ten new little friends!

'Good', the caretaker went on. 'I see you would like that. But *you* couldn't carry them. I'll bring them round for you. Where do you live?'

'I don't know.'

'What's that? You don't know your own address?'

'No. I live at the home of Herr Sesemann and his daughter Clara.'

The caretaker smiled. He knew where Clara's home was.

'Off you go, then; and don't lose the kittens on the way. I'll bring the other ones round to-morrow.'

When she got back Heidi met with a cool reception. Fräulein Rottenmeier was in a furious temper: they had been looking for Heidi since mid-day. They all thought there must have been an accident. Still, now that the little scatterbrain was back, they sat down to their meal.

In the middle of supper, the three of them were surprised at hearing some strange little cries.

'Heidi, what on earth is that noise?'

'It's not me ... it's the cats.'

'Cats! Cats! Goodness gracious me! What a state of affairs!'

And Fräulein Emma, who hated the pretty little creatures, was just able to find the strength to leave the table, to take refuge in the library and to call out:

'Gaspard, Gaspard, throw them out into the street!'

The servant, who really loved cats and who did not object to making fun of the terrible governess, took care not to obey her. He noticed Clara's pleading look.

'Never fear, Miss. I'll make them a soft nest in a room into which Fräulein Rottenmeier never pokes her nose.'

'Oh, thank you, Gaspard dear!'

Heidi didn't dare tell Clara that the two little kittens would soon be followed by some more.

Next day, right in the middle of one of the tutor's lessons, the little organ grinder appeared at the front door.

'Good morning, Sir,' he said to Gaspard. 'I've come to get the pennies Miss promised me.'

'What pennies? What Miss?'

Their argument made such a noise that Clara could hear every word they said. She was bright, so she guessed that the 'Miss' could only be Heidi.

'Oh, it's someone who plays a hurdy-gurdy, Sir. Let him play us a tune, it's such fun.'

The poor Professor raised his eyes to heaven. What else might happen in a house where such things could take place?

Hardly had the music begun than it was interrupted by the furious arrival of Fräulein Rottenmeier.

'What does this hubbub mean? Who has given this little rascal permission to . . . ?'

On the wooden floor a strange flat creature could be seen creeping along and looking inquisitively at the governess's boots. The tortoise was fascinated by the soft, bright leather.

'Away with it. Throw the ragamuffin and his tortoise into the
street. Goodness me! It will be the death of me. ...'

Gaspard, who could hardly stop himself from laughing, made
a sign to the boy that the joke had gone far enough. He led him
to the front door, slipping him ten pence on the way.

'That's payment enough for your music, my lad. But see you
don't come back here in a hurry.'

The tutor went on with the lesson where it had been interrupted, while Fräulein Rottenmeier, who had decided to keep
an eye on them, surveyed them crossly. Not for long, however!
Gaspard soon reappeared, a wicker basket held carefully in his
arms.

'This is for Mademoiselle Clara, I'm told.'

'Put it in a corner, Gaspard, and don't let us have any more
disturbances.'

But Clara, who was usually so hard-working, could not stop herself from now and then stealing a glance in the direction of the mysterious parcel. The tutor grew impatient.

'Miss Clara, just see once and for all what is in that basket, then we can get on with our lessons.'

Clara lifted up the cover. Ten little pussies made their escape from the basket. The little balls of fur tumbled round the room, clinging on to the curtains and climbing up the Professor's long legs. More dead than alive, Fräulein Rottenmeier jumped up onto the table.

'Help! Help! Gaspard, Gaspard, save me!'

The butler dashed in. In a few moments he had the kittens back in their basket.

'Throw them into the street. Ough!'

But Gaspard would have none of it. Encouraged by the furtive smiles of the two young ladies, he took the tribe of kittens to the 'secret room'. But you may be sure that Emma Rottenmeier knew nothing about that.

Heidi's violin

Heidi's Grandfather did not have to wait too long before his grand-daughter came back to the village of Dörfli. After a few months in Frankfurt, Heidi returned to the Alp, its flowers, its pure air and its fir trees.

The years had passed by, and now signs of winter were appearing in the high-up Alp: the first snowflakes had already fallen on the autumn crocuses. When the icy wind began to blow among the fir trees, Grandfather decided that the time had come for them to move down to the village.

'To-morrow', he said to Heidi, 'we shall collect the goats and the kid and we shall take advantage of the hospitality which kind Dr Braun has offered us.'

Heidi agreed with the old man's decision, but she was sad, all the same, at the thought of leaving her nice chalet. She went out for a last walk to say good-bye to the mountain. The feeble sun hardly warmed her. It was autumn.

Heidi was now twelve. She was no longer a little girl. Her Grandfather, seeing her dark plaits wrap themselves round her head when she shook it, still thought of her as a five-year-old, an age when she had been mischievous and headstrong and with as curly a head of hair as the kid's. The years had gone by and all the sad and all the pleasant things that had happened during that time had gone with them.

Clara, Heidi's great friend at Frankfurt, was now no longer an invalid. Loving care and attention, a stay in the beautiful countryside at Maïenfield, the affection of everyone round her: all these things had helped to give back to her the use of her legs. So Heidi felt no regret at having been exiled for a while with Clara in the big, grey, cold town, for there she had made a wonderful friend; now that Clara was cured, her happiness was almost complete.

But what a terrible sadness it was when Grandmother died! At least the old lady had passed away peacefully, surrounded by the tender affection of her family. Little Peter had turned into a sensible, hard-working boy. Brigitte had always been devoted to the old Grandmother, Uncle was always kind and attentive towards her, and Heidi read beautifully to her from the prayer-book.

But now that Grandmother was no longer with them, life still went on. The doctor took Brigitte into service in Dörfli and found a job for Peter as a gardener at Ragaz.

The doctor and Uncle had become great friends. Together they planned and built a great house, the finest in the village. The doctor lived there all the time; there he had his flat and his surgery. But there were also rooms for Heidi and her Grandfather to live in during the winter. At the back of the house a fine stable had been built for the goats.

The doctor, who was Heidi's godfather and gave her lessons, had put aside one room as a little study for Heidi. Here she is at the little desk where she liked to read and write while the doctor was at work. Her school books are in rows on the shelves which run along the wall.

In the big room, where a fire leapt and danced in the grate, Grandfather sat smoking his pipe in an easy chair.

Together they made a happy family, and Brigitte felt proud when she saw how Heidi had learned from her how to look after the house and garden.

Outside, the whole world seemed to be asleep beneath the snow. But how good it was to be inside the quiet and peaceful house.

Someone was knocking at the door: three knocks that were so timid that only Heidi heard them. A little boy was standing outside; he seemed very unhappy.

'Come in, George. Don't stay out there catching cold.'

'No. I don't want to come in.'

'How's that?'

'I don't want to.'

'Come in, little chap. If we leave the door open the cold air will go right through the house. Is your mother still sick?'

'Yes. The doctor must see her.'

'My godfather will visit your mother and he will soon make her better. In the meanwhile, you sit down by the fire.'

The little boy drew near the fireplace while the doctor got ready as quickly as he could. Soon, they went off together into the cold, black night. The doctor took George's little paw in his big hand and held it tight so as to warm it.

When they had gone Heidi sat down near her Grandfather, who was thoughtfully drawing on his pipe.

'Do you think George's mother is going to die, Grandfather?'

'I very much hope she won't. Your godfather will do all he can to save her. But if she *should* die, how sad that will be for her husband and children. Poor Theresa is still a young girl. She would have altogether too much on her hands if she were to have to take her mother's place and look after the family.'

'To be a doctor like my godfather is a wonderful profession, don't you think so, Grandfather? I should like to be like him, but it must be very hard to become a doctor.'

'You can work with sick people even if you are not a doctor. Many girls like you become nurses and some are sisters in hospitals.'

'Well then, I should like to be a nurse and help the doctor.'

'There's time enough to think about that, Heidi dear. Just now you must go up to bed.'

Heidi gave her Grandfather a kiss and went up to her room.

She loved her little bedroom, it was so cheerful and clean. The walls were panelled half-way up in light maple wood and the top half was gaily painted with coloured flowers on a white background. Rhododendrons, jonquils, crocuses: it was as

though the alpine meadow had re-established itself on the walls of the room. On the bed lay a big eiderdown decorated in large red and white squares. The cupboard in which Heidi put her things, the table and the chair were made of pine. Well waxed and polished, they shone faintly in the dusk. Happy at being in so cheerful a room, Heidi slipped between the covers of her bed and was soon asleep.

She had been asleep for more than an hour before the doctor returned home again. He seemed thoughtful.

'It's really bad, then?' Grandfather asked him with real concern.

'Bad? No, but serious enough. The poor woman must be taken to the hospital at Maïenfeld. With rest and care she should be all right.'

'But who will look after the children? Is there nothing we can do?'

'It's hard to say. Their father is there. He doesn't want anyone else to come into the house and he says he will do everything himself. It is hard to understand him.'

'Let us hope God will come to his aid', Grandfather said. 'Good-night, doctor.'

Next day the doctor paid another visit to the sick woman. Two hours later he returned, looking gloomy.

'I have arranged for her to go to Maïenfeld,' he explained. 'It was the only sensible thing to do. But I am worried about Theresa. She is so young to have to look after her father and her two brothers. And then, whilst George is a good, well-behaved boy, I can't say as much for Tony, the elder of the two. While we were getting things ready, he simply stood still and looked on.'

Heidi had put on her wooden clogs and had her hooded cape over her head. 'I'm going to help Theresa', she said.

'Don't go there yet, Heidi. It's a kind thought, and you have a warm heart, but just now it's better to leave the poor man alone with the children. You can go later, say this afternoon when school is over.'

'Yes, Grandfather, you are quite right.'

As they were coming out of school, Heidi caught hold of Theresa's shawl.

'Theresa, would you like me to help you at home?'

'Help to do what? I can't do anything. I don't know a thing about it.'

'Hasn't your mother taught you?'

'She didn't want to. She said I was too clumsy.'

'All right then, now it's time to learn. Come along, Theresa.

We'll manage, the pair of us, to do the housework and the cooking.'

The house was in a sad state. The plates and the glasses from the mid-day meal were still on the table. The room hadn't been swept out and the beds were still un-made. But where should they make a start? Heidi thought for a moment and then she came to a decision:

'Theresa, you make the beds. I'll light the fire; and while we are laying the table, the flames will be warming the house. When your father comes back you can help me get supper ready.'

'Oh, yes, Heidi. If you show me what to do I'll do it quick enough.'

While the two girls were busying themselves, Tony opened the door and then stood quite still in the middle of the room.

'What are you doing there?'

'Oh Tony!' exclaimed Heidi, 'look what you have done! You did not dry your boots before coming indoors. There are two big puddles around your legs.'

'What's that to you? You are not in charge here.'

'You're a bad boy. You would do better to help us instead of talking like that.'

'No, I'm a man. It's Theresa who should be doing mother's work.'

And out he went, banging the door behind him.

Little George, whom Heidi had set down at the kitchen table to peel the potatoes for supper, was proud of the work he was doing. The quarrel upset him.

'Tony is a naughty boy', he said, gulping as though to stop himself from crying.

'No, he's upset', Heidi replied.

Just then Tony returned. He seemed to be sorry and he walked right round the kitchen without saying a word. Heidi was too tactful to seem to be aware of anything amiss.

'Tony!' she said. 'Would you fetch some wood for the fire? It's too heavy for me to carry.'

The boy went off at once. He was glad to do this man's job and soon came back with a big armful of dry wood.

Grandfather had come to look for Heidi. When he opened the front door a fine sight met his eyes. The table was laid; a cheerful blaze lit up the hearth. Seated in front of the fire, Theresa was reading her lesson books, and the two boys were playing a game at the end of the table. Grandfather looked at the scene steadily for a moment and then he said to Tony:

'Everything is in order. Your father can come home now with an easy mind, and your mother would be happy to know that the house is being so well looked after. What do you say, Sergeant?'

The boy sat up straight. He was proud that the old gentleman had spoken to *him* and that he had called him 'Sergeant'.

'Well done, Theresa. Well done, George, for peeling the potatoes. See you to-morrow, Tony. I hope I shall be able to congratulate you too then.'

Tony bowed his head. He understood that he would have to

work just like the others. And, sure enough, he did so. Every day for two weeks Heidi helped Theresa to look after the house and do the cooking. All this time their mother grew better. By the middle of January, the doctor said, she would be able to return home. While they waited for her, they got ready for Christmas.

'Still twenty days', Heidi sighed. 'I wish it was now. Have you thought about presents?'

'No', Tony replied. 'We haven't done anything yet.'

'It's not hard. I'll help you and so will my Grandfather. I'll go and ask him.'

Every evening when school was over the house became as busy as a bee-hive. Each of the children was determined to produce a masterpiece. Helped by Brigitte, Heidi embroidered a comfortable cushion for her Grandfather. Theresa was making one too, for her mother. Heidi was drawing an almanac for her Godfather. Little George was also making one, but instead of drawing the pictures himself, as Heidi was doing, he cut them out of an old almanac and stuck them down on a sheet of white paper. For her friend Clara, Heidi intended to make a basket. Grandfather decided to teach Tony how to weave wicker-work too. He was going to make a fine bread-basket for his mother.

December passed so quickly that Christmas Eve was on them before they were aware of it.

A few days earlier Heidi and her uncle had gone for a walk in the forest. There they chose a little fir tree, leafy and upright, which they set up in the doctor's big room and covered with decorations and candles. In front of the tree Theresa and her brothers placed a cut-out of Baby Jesus in His cradle.

Now they awaited midnight. They were all gathered around the fire: the doctor, Heidi, Brigitte, Theresa, the two boys, and their father too. In his deep voice Grandfather sang the lovely carol:

Noël, Noël,
The angels did say.

Suddenly Brigitte stood up and ran towards the door.
'I heard someone knock.'

The door opened and a handsome young man walked in. He clasped Brigitte in his arms and kissed her on both cheeks. It was Peter, who had returned from Ragaz to pass the Christmas festival with his family.

'Happy Christmas, Mother! Happy Christmas everyone!'

'And now', said Heidi, 'I'm going to give out the presents.'
Everyone fell silent. Little George was sucking his thumb, looking at the ceiling and moving from one leg to the other. He wanted to open his presents immediately. But where had they gone to? Heidi had arranged them beautifully under the branches of the Christmas tree. But they were no longer there!

At this moment of crisis the Grandfather got up and left the room. He said that he had left his favourite pipe upstairs in his bedroom and he must go and fetch it.

What on earth was happening? Heidi was really put-out; such preparations for the day, such lovely presents! She felt like crying. But then there came a knock at the door.

Tony retreated with a secret smile into a corner.

It seemed that only he knew what was going on. He half-opened the folding door and there entered a wonderful Father Christmas in a magnificent red cloak and hood. Father Christmas grasped a small bundle of long, dry twigs. On his back there was a basket overflowing with many-coloured packages.

'Good-day, children. Are there any rascals among yoú? If there are, I've brought these twigs to beat them with.'

And Father Christmas shook his bundle. But you could see from the merry look in his eye that he had no intention of carrying out his threat.

'All right, then, as there are only good children and good parents here I'm going to empty my basket and give out my presents. I'll be glad to put it down. It's too heavy for my old back.'

Everyone was given his parcel. They all kissed one another. There were some tears. Father Christmas put a long black box into Heidi's arms and said: 'It's from Clara.'

'Father Christmas', the doctor said, 'wouldn't you like us to sing a carol in your honour?'

'Yes, yes, please do. I'll join in.'

In the middle of all this excitement Grandfather took off his red cloak and, followed by the others, began to sing:

Silent night
Holy night
All is calm
All is bright

Theresa, George and Tony recited poems to the doctor which Heidi had taught them; he was highly appreciative. They were nervous and they hesitated a little, but everyone congratulated them.

Then, when the last candle on the Christmas tree had spluttered out, the young people went upstairs to bed. Left alone in the room, Heidi admired the beautiful violin, in its long, black case, which Clara had given her. What a wonderful present!

As she slept, she dreamed she was playing on it the lively tunes of the valley and the hymns which, not so long ago, Grandmother had taught her to love.